TIPS

1. DON'T DRAW ATTENTION TO YOURSELF.

SERIOUSLY, DON'T FORGET THE SNACKS.

2. QUESTION EVERYTHING.

Is this a clue?

3. PRACTICE YOUR THINKING POSE.

Hmm...

Hmm...

hmm...

Are you a clue?

Am I a clue?

4. BE A GOOD LISTENER.

WHAT?

EVERYTHING!

5. ASK TOUGH QUESTIONS.

What sound does a cat make?

Meow!

6. BLEND IN WITH THE LOCALS.

Coo!

Coo!

Coo!

ARE YOU READY TO SOLVE YOUR FIRST CASE?

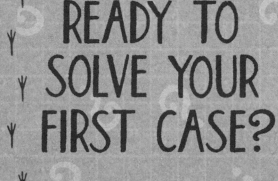

THE DAILY QUI

HAWKEYE HAMILTON

BEAKY GARRILL

The Corrections Dept.

Flaming O's CANDLE EMPORIUM

The corrections department would like to apologize for a typographical error in yesterday's issue. Readers were led to believe that the Bird-Drain Bath Company could assist with pluming problems. This is not the case. We apolologize for any contusion clawed

FOR MY GRANDAD
who loved detective stories; my **sister**, who likes them; **and my brother**, whose opinion remains a mystery... & JONNY

Chloe · Rayna · Jackson · Ben · Isla

CLARION BOOKS
3 PARK AVENUE
NEW YORK, NEW YORK 10016
COPYRIGHT © 2017 BY MEG McLAREN
FIRST PUBLISHED IN THE UNITED KINGDOM IN 2017 BY ANDERSEN PRESS.
PUBLISHED IN THE UNITED STATES IN 2017.

CLARION BOOKS IS AN IMPRINT OF HOUGHTON MIFFLIN HARCOURT PUBLISHING COMPANY.
www.hmhco.com
THE TEXT WAS SET IN JOSEFIN SANS.
THE ILLUSTRATIONS IN THIS BOOK WERE DONE USING DIGITAL MEDIA.
LIBRARY OF CONGRESS CATALOGING-IN-PUBLICATION DATA IS AVAILABLE.
ISBN 978-1-328-71561-6

CULTURE VULTURE
Your guide to this season's latest trends

CLARION BOOKS

HOUGHTON MIFFLIN HARCOURT ★ BOSTON NEW YORK

PIGEON P.I.

PRIVATE INVESTIGATORS

DON'T COME MORE HARD-BOILED THAN THIS!

WE'LL CRACK ANY CASE

WRITTEN AND ILLUSTRATED BY

★ MEG McLAREN ★

Business was slow,
just the way I liked it.

My partner, Stanley, had skipped town a while back, so I'd decided to take things easy.

But then the kid showed up.

She'd been here for a while.

It was time to find out why.

The kid and her friends had come to the city ready for adventure, but they'd found danger instead . . .

She had escaped,
but her friends hadn't
been so lucky.

MISSING
PET RUBINO BOURKE PARROT
"RUBY"

MILK

MISSING
PET BUDGERIGAR
"JIMMY"

LAST SEEN IN HIS CAGE OUTSIDE HIS
LIKES: GARDENING
LOVES: CROONERS, LIBRARY QU
DISLIKES: LISTS
IF SIGHTED, PLEASE CALL

No one had seen them since.

I told her I didn't take cases anymore.

But she was pretty convincing.

"Come back tomorrow and we'll talk," I said. But she didn't.

The police were busy on a big case. I'd have to do this alone.

News travels fast
in this town, especially
the bad kind.

Word on the wire
was that birds had been
going missing all over.

All the evidence pointed to the Red Herring Bar and Grill as the thief's hideout.

It was time to take a closer look.

It didn't take
me long.

This little canary already
had a plan. She just needed
the pin from my hat.

The kid turned out to be a genius at picking locks.
Everything was going well until . . .

The villainous feather thief was shouting orders.
I couldn't leave now—I was so close to the truth.

As usual, my curiosity got the better of me.
The missing birds made it out safely,

but it looked like
my wings were
clipped for good.

THESE HEAVIES
ARE HEAVIER
THAN THEY LOOK!

WHOOPS!

She's my partner, after all.

With another jailbird behind bars, the streets were safe again.

And we planned to keep them that way.

ADVANCED DETECTION

MISSING
GOLDEN EGG
CALL: G. GOOSE

I've made an egg-citing discovery!

Egg-cellent work!

HAVE A WITTY LINE READY WHEN YOU SOLVE YOUR CASE.

DISCUSS IDEAS WITH YOUR PARTNER.

What if...?

No. How about..?

No. But then we could...

I don't think so. What if we..?

YES!

PRACTICE TAKING NOTES.

TRY TO REMEMBER WHEN THINGS HAPPEN AND IN WHAT ORDER.

Hmm...

Vee's notes
7:30 Woke up
7:31 Got up
7:40 Ate apple for breakfast
8:00 Murray woke up
8:01 Murray reports his apple missing
8:02 THE SEARCH BEGINS!

FAMOUS DETECTIVES

LIEUTENANT COLUMBA
(COLUMBA LEGATUS)

J.B. FLEDGLING

BONJOUR!

MONSIEUR PARROT

MISS MARBLE-D WOOD QUAIL

SHERSTORK HOLMES

DUCK TRACY